THE STORY OF SANGA
THE TALE OF AN AFRICAN CHILD.

Written by Damian Chukwurah Amazu

Illustrated by John Stine Obiechina

Edited by Cynthia Calzone

Published by Creative Mind & Thinker Books

Copyright ©2022 by Damian Chukwurah Amazu

All Rights Reserved.

Any of the content in this book cannot be used or reproduced without the prior permission of the author, illustrator and publisher.

ISBN: 978-1-7369433-5-9

Email: Creativemindandthinkerbooks@gmail.com

For order and other details, please contact the above information. Special discounts are also available.

Dedication

I dedicate this book to all the wonderful children who are intelligent, brave, courageous, and determined to be literate in life. Also, to all the great children who respect their parents, and willing to achieve greater goals in the future.

Respect

I respect and acknowledge all my readers and wish you tremendous success in life.

About the Book

Sanga was determined to become a prominent personality in the society and willing to help his community. After conceiving a dream for greatness, he asked several questions and faced many challenges in the process. Nevertheless, with sheer determination and the support of his parents, he achieved his dream.

It is an interesting work of literature for every young person with great dreams that can be achieved through strength, determination, and hard work, as shown in this masterpiece.

Chapter 1
Sanga and his Mother.

Sanga and his mother were having a discussion after lunch, and he began telling his mother that he would like to be famous someday.

"Mum, what can I do to become famous?" the boy asked.

"Son, you need to be educated first," his mother answered as she smiled.

Sanga asked his mum again, "But how can I do that?"

His mother retorted, "Son, you should start going to school."

Sanga still wanted to know more, so he asked further. "When and where?"

His mother softly replied with a smile, "Son, when you are ready, I will take you to a place where you can enroll in school."

Sanga joyfully accepted the offer and replied immediately, "Mother, I am ready now."

Sanga's mother was surprised at Sanga's sudden readiness. "Did you just make up your mind now?" she asked.

"Yes, mother. I am ready now," Sanga replied.

His mother promised to take him to the place where he would be enrolled after she discussed this conversation with her husband. Sanga embraced his mother with smiles all over his face.

Chapter 2
Sanga and his Parents.

In Sanga's community, education was quite unpopular because his people were known as hunters, and none of their ancestors had ever been to school. Although they heard about educated people, they had never given any consideration or thought to it.

Later in the evening, when Sanga's father returned from hunting, Sanga's mother briefed her husband about her discussion with their son. His father was astonished like his mother was earlier during her discussion with Sanga. So, they decided to summon Sanga and talk with him to understand if that was what he wanted. Sanga's father began by telling him about what his mother had said. He then asked Sanga what motivated him to accept the offer without thinking twice or reflecting on it and what would happen to his hunting?

Sanga told him that he had always wanted to be famous and do something different in life; this made him ask his mum what he could do to become famous. In addition, the moment she told him that education was the key to actualizing his dream, he did not need to think or sleep on it for any reason whatsoever. He simply decided to change to a new career. He also told them about his friend, Zuma, from the neighboring community, his former hunting partner. Zuma now looks and behaves differently, and he no longer looks unkempt.

"Each time I walked with him in our community, people praised and hailed him," Sanga said. "He has completely changed. One day, I asked Zuma about the secret of his success, and he told me the same thing my mum said to me during our conversation earlier today that "education is the key". The moment mum said education was the answer, I remembered my interaction with Zuma. Since that meeting with Zuma, I had always wanted to be like him so that I could be different from other people in our community," Sanga added.

Sanga's parents were so happy to hear this, and they promised to give him their best support. His mum told him that they should set out early for the journey to enable them arrive at the school in time since it was about 7 miles away from their home.

Chapter 3
Journey to School.

The next morning, Sanga and his mother left very early to the school where he would be registered. He was finally enrolled, and his mother left him in the school and returned home.

Sanga's first day in school was full of confusion because he could not even pronounce his name properly as he should, like the other students. To make matters worse, he was very unkempt. Other students began making fun of him, but he ignored them and remained silent.

At the end of the day, Sanga walked back home after school. This took him about one and half hours because there was no means of transportation. It was difficult since the journey was long and lonely, but Sanga had decided not to let anything deter him from achieving his dream.

Chapter 4
At Home.

When Sanga got home, his parents embraced him. Then, they asked him if he had any difficulties in the class and walking back home from school. When Sanga told his parents everything that happened both in the class and on his way home, his mother started crying, but Sanga's father asked her to stop else Sanga might be discouraged out of pity for her.

"Son, you are now an ambitious man. Men like you always have a history book about their suffering and triumph." He further explained to him that there was no success without ugly stories. Therefore, he should cheer up and continue with the ambition to achieve his dream. Sanga thanked his parents and excused himself to his room to get some rest.

Chapter 5
Mockery.

Sanga became the topic of mockery at school because he still had difficulties catching up with his school activities. His interaction with people in the school environment was also awkward as Sanga had no idea how to interact with people outside his small community. Other students were not friendly toward him at all; they treated Sanga like a strange ghost that appeared from the moon. The teachers would caution the students whenever Sanga was ill-treated.

Despite all these experiences, Sanga remained determined. Sometimes after school, some teachers would call Sanga and advise him not to relent, telling him not to give up on achieving his dream. However, Sanga would always thank them with a smile and promised never to disappoint them.

Some of his neighbors also made fun of him each time they see him return from school. However, Sanga overlooked their actions and promised himself that he would reach the mountain's top. He was encouraged by the thought that those who mocked him would someday sing a different tune about him.

Chapter 6
Sanga's Performance and Lifestyle.

After several months, Sanga's lifestyle changed. He started dressing formally and became very neat. His performance in class greatly improved, and now other students envied him. He could write and pronounce many words correctly, unlike before.

He scored high in class works and had excellent grades in examinations. His performance called the attention of the school administration. In a bid to encourage him, he was awarded for the best performance and most brilliant student of the term. That became a steppingstone to a greater height for Sanga's dream; he was so happy and delighted at his success.

When Sanga got home that afternoon, he disclosed the success story to his parents. They were happy and quite proud of him.

Chapter 7
Sanga gets a Scholarship.

When Sanga finished elementary school, he was given a scholarship to high school. He did not stop there; he kept moving forward and winning numerous awards. They include the best English writing student, outstanding essay writer, and Most Valuable Student (MVS) awards. His parents were extremely proud of him and his achievements.

Yet, people in his neighborhood still did not see the need and value for education. Instead, they were satisfied with their hunting.

Sanga was determined and continuously had his parents' help and support, which gave him the courage to succeed in all his academic pursuits. After his excellent performance in his high school final examination, Sanga was offered another scholarship to pursue his United Mobutu States University career. He was elated. His parents could not believe that their poor son was heading toward becoming an important personality in the society.

Chapter 8
Good News.

When his relatives and friends in the neighborhood heard about Sanga's success story, they marveled and started asking him numerous questions.

"How many days do you need to walk to get to United Mobutu States University?" "Would you swim?"

They had heard much about United Mobutu States University. It was a fine and lovely place, so they wanted to know how he would make it there. Finally, Sanga told them that he would fly.

"Would you fly on an eagle for the trip?" they asked him further.

"I will travel in an airplane and not on an eagle because eagles do not carry people," Sanga explained.

"What is an airplane?" they asked.

"It is an object that makes a loud noise while flying in the air. It usually scares us whenever we see it in the sky," Sanga explained.

"Do you mean that object that looks like a bird, that makes us run and hide inside our houses and bushes each time it is flying in the sky?" one of them asked.

Sanga nodded and echoed, "Yes." At this time, they all became envious of him, forgetting that they were mocking him before.

Chapter 9
At the Airport.

When Sanga and his parents got to the airport, his mum hugged him and started crying. His father tried to console her and persuaded her to stop, or it might affect Sanga's emotions. Sanga's parents began to advise him, reminding him of his humble background and what he was going to pursue. They reminded him of the goal he would actualize if he could remain serious with his studies.

"My son, promise me that you will not become a bad person or join bad groups when you get to the United Mobutu States University," his mother remarked, sounding agitated. Sanga retorted and sincerely promised his parents that he would certainly retain his integrity. Finally, they hugged him once again before separating in tears and bade him farewell. Then, Sanga boarded his flight to begin his journey for a better future.

Chapter 10
Sanga's Trip.

Sanga had never flown on an airplane before. However, since there was no airport in his community, Sanga traveled miles with his parents to another community to board the airplane.

Everything was like a movie to him, he could hardly understand the pilot's, passengers, or air hostess accent, but being a smart gent, he quietly kept calm and watched what other passengers were doing. He paid attention by looking at other passengers and imitating whatever they did after the pilot, or air hostesses made an announcement.

He was also hoping to see someone who could speak his language or had a similar English accent like him, but no one like that ever showed up, so he was a little bit disappointed. All he could do was to remain silent until he got to his destination.

Chapter 11
United Mobutu State Airport.

Before Sanga left his community, he was given instructions on how he would retrieve his luggage after going through the airport checks; and the documents to submit, and exactly what to say to the immigration and customs officers. Sanga followed the instructions carefully and finally made his way out after all the procedures.

When Sanga stepped out of the arrival terminal, he was surprised as he saw a man holding up a post with his name boldly written, "Welcome, Sanga." He walked up to the man, introduced himself. The man also introduced himself as a staff member of the United Mobutu States University. After exchanging pleasantries, they boarded the school bus and zoomed off. Unfortunately, the University staff member barely understood Sanga's accent, nor was Sanga able to clearly grasp what the man and other students on the bus were saying. However, it was a fun time all around.

Chapter 12
In the Classroom.

The first day in class was quite challenging for Sanga; he could barely understand what the instructors and lecturers said. During the classes' general short introduction session, the students hardly understood his accent. Sanga would have to pay extra close attention and watch their eyes and body language to grasp what they were saying. Sometimes his assumptions would fail him; other times, they would be right. Despite all these challenges, he was never discouraged nor disturbed. Sanga was so happy to have met different races, accents, cultures, and backgrounds. They all sat together, sharing ideas and smiling.

Sanga was in the department of Basic Medical Sciences at the United Mobutu States University. He decided to become a medical doctor so he could go back and help his people since he would be the first medical doctor in the history of his community. Sanga became friendly with other students as he progressed in the school and was loved by many. The lecturers and some students did not mock him. Instead, they helped him when other students were using him as the topic of their discussions.

"That's life for you; not all will like you, and neither will all hate you," one of his lecturers encouraged him. Sanga realized that life in United Mobutu State was far different, including the weather and culture, but he adjusted to all these factors.

Chapter 13
A new Friend.

Baringo, Sanga's classmate, was very interested in knowing more about Sanga's background and how he came to study at United Mobutu State University. However, he did not really want his friendship but wanted to see facts he could use to mock him.

As they were walking down the aisle in the school one day, Baringo asked, "Do you sleep in a house where you came from?"

Sanga looked at him in awe and answered, "No, we don't; we live in a thick forest with trees and animals."

Baringo was amazed and said, "What! Are you serious?" Baringo could not believe it. "And those wild animals living in the bush do not use you as their meal?" Baringo questioned.

Sanga, showing no hint of doubt or reservation, added, "We even play, dine, and sleep with all those wild animals, especially lions, leopards, and tigers."

Baringo was utterly astonished and thrown off balance. He asked Sanga another question. "How did you get to United Mobutu State University, and how did you know about the school?"

Sanga replied courageously, though sarcastically, "Because we are friendly with eagles, they flew me here with the help of their wings. I was awarded a scholarship to study here at United Mobutu State University."

Baringo's eyebrows were standing upright because Sanga's answers were unbelievable. Baringo bowed out disappointedly. The only thing he could utter was, "Our instructors never told us that eagles could convey people from place to place."

Sanga simply replied, "Your instructors must not know everything and have never been to all parts of the world. Maybe you have forgotten that this was said to you?"

Sanga advised him to ask his instructors about what he had told him next time, and Baringo nodded in acceptance. Sanga had succeeded in putting away the one who had intended to mock him.

Chapter 14
Awards.

Sanga received many awards for his outstanding performances. He was awarded the best academia of the school and the most brilliant student of all time. He did his assignments, tests, projects, and examinations on time and received excellent marks in all his subjects.

After several years of academic studies and internships, Sanga graduated as a qualified Medical Practitioner. Then, he was awarded another scholarship to obtain his master's degree and Ph.D. in medicine. After all these achievements, he worked for a while to gain experience in his field. Finally, he decided to go home and establish a standard health care facility in his community.

Chapter 15
Sanga`s Returns.

Sanga's return was announced to his community. The neighboring communities were also present to welcome him. He had become a popular professional among his people and the other communities. The arena was filled with people waiting patiently for his arrival.

When Sanga finally arrived in his neighborhood, none of his relatives could even recognize him. His parents, especially, saw great changes in his appearance. Everything about him had changed tremendously, his voice, complexion, attire, and movement. His parents were so happy to see him; they embraced him tightly. His mother broke into tears of joy as Sanga hugged her.

He was welcomed like a president. The entire community gathered in glee, and Sanga addressed them in good time. Then, he retired to his parent's house to have some much-needed rest after his long trip.

Chapter 16
Brief Speech.

Sanga summoned his community and the neighboring communities to share his experiences and future goals. His purpose was to encourage them on the importance of education. He began by telling them his experiences, starting from the mockeries he received from his friends even while he was still with them in the community and at United Mobutu State University.

He explained to them that despite all the odds and ugly experiences, he was able to achieve his goal. Sanga finally made his parents and himself proud. He chose to ignore the hard times and focused more on the future, which has earned him everything he had achieved. He encouraged them to enroll in school and acquire education, and most importantly, never give up on their goals in life.

He equally told them about his profession and advised them that they needn't have to travel miles anymore for medical care. From now on, Sanga would be their community physician. He told them of his plans to build a standard health care center.

There was a tumultuous cheer, the crowd happily began to sing songs of praises composed in his name, and they lifted him from his feet.

Chapter 17
Fulfilled Dream.

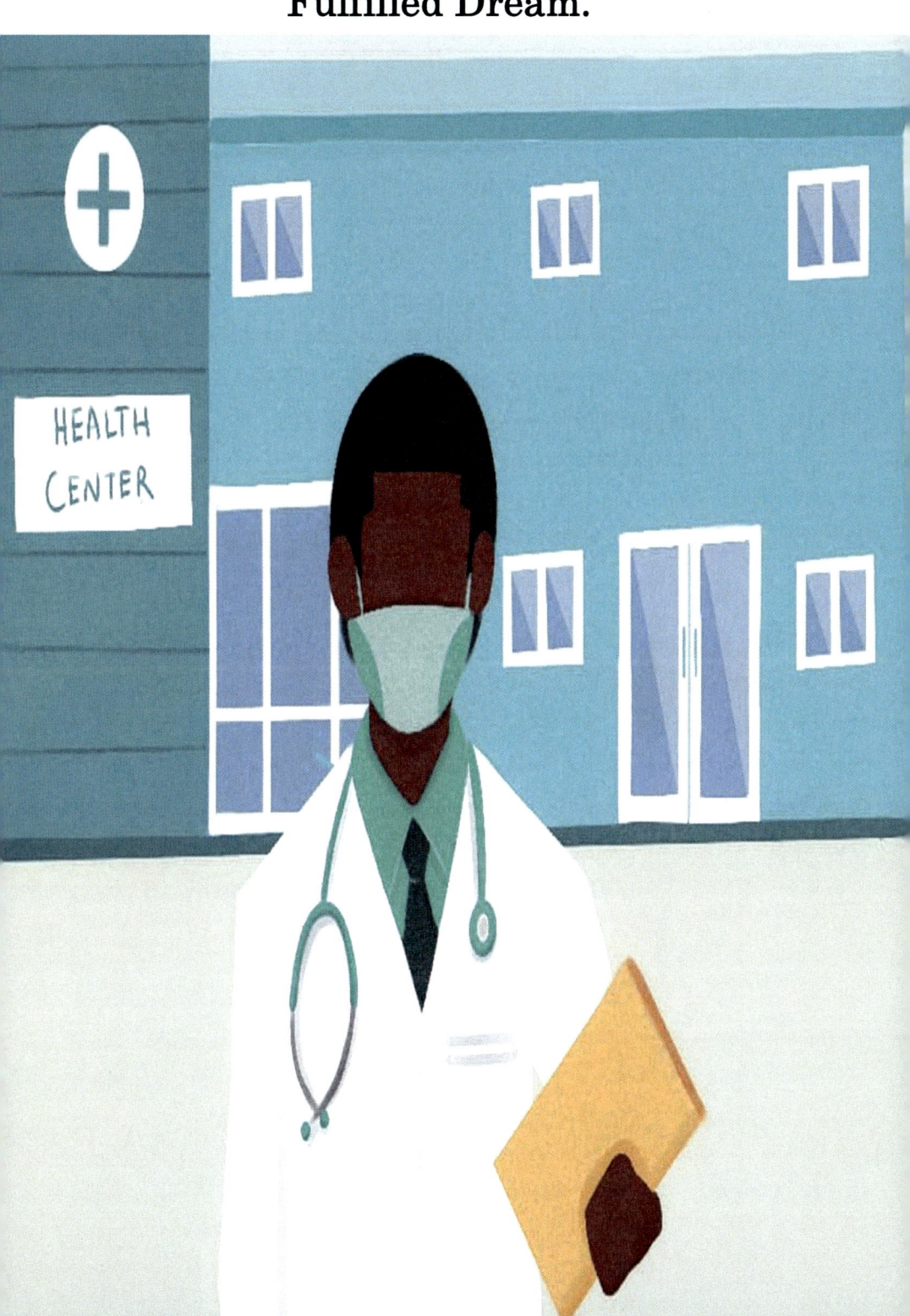

Sanga finally completed the building project and named the health care center after his mother. Sanga began to take good care of his people; he became their medical consultant, taught them the necessary medical exercises for therapy, and performed evaluations himself. Patients within and outside the community were coming to his hospital for medical care.

Sanga continued to make his people see the importance of education. He became a rare gem, and within six months, many parents had enrolled their children in school. Sanga built some schools as well and employed teachers from afar to educate his people and anybody who wanted to learn. Sanga fulfilled his dreams, and he became a great man and mentor. He transformed the lives of his people. As a result, he was given the title of "The Man Greater Than Men."

Advise.

Dreams achieved gladden the heart. Therefore, ensure to work hard toward your dream and not be dismayed when it becomes tough or difficult. It is better to conquer your fears and succeed than to blame yourself for not trying and failing to achieve your dreams.

Questions.

Who was Sanga?

What was his dream?

What award did he receive in his elementary school?

What was his first scholarship?

What were the awards he won while in United Mobutu States University?

What did he use to travel to United Mobutu States University?

What were his major challenges when he got to United Mobutu States University?

Who became his friend at United Mobutu States University?

What did Sanga build in his community?

What name did the community give him?

Who encouraged Sanga from the beginning?

What was Sanga's profession when he returned from the United Mobutu State University?

How many degrees does Sanga have?

What was Sanga's career/profession before he became a student?

Who motivated Sanga into going to school?

Provide the answers here.

WHAT DID YOU LEARN FROM THE STORY?

Made in the USA
Monee, IL
08 March 2023